THE RAINBOW ORCHID

VOLUME THREE

GAREN EWING

EGMONT

EGMONT

We bring stories to life

First published 2012 by Egmont UK Limited, 239 Kensington High Street, London W8 6SA

ISBN 978 1 4052 5599 8

1 3 5 7 9 10 8 6 4 2

Printed in Singapore

46834/1

EGMONT LUCKY COIN

Our story began over a century ago, when seventeen-year-old Egmont Harald Petersen found a coin in the street.

He was on his way to buy a flyswatter, a small hand-operated printing machine that he then set up in his tiny apartment.

The coin brought him such good luck that today Egmont has offices in over 30 countries around the world. And that lucky coin is still kept at the company's head offices in Denmark.

Mr Drubbin - ESB field agent

Sir Alfred Catesby-Grey – historical researcher

Julius Chancer – historical-research assistant

Lily Lawrence – silent-film actress

Nathaniel Crumpole – movie publicity agent

Upjanu - Urvatjan High Strategos

Makshjia - Queen of Urvatja

Meru - retainer to Father Pinkleton

Gozavu - Keeper of Urvatja

Majaa - Keeper's apprentice

Scobie - butler

Newton – botanist

Urkaz Grope – businessman

Evelyn Crow – personal assistant to Urkaz Grope

Box – pugilist and henchman

James Palfrey - musicologist

Bert - Wembley Exhibition guide

Lord Reginald Lawrence - aristocrat

Perkins - gardener

Nellie - housemaid

Tobias Starling - police Inspector

Eloise Tayaut – aerobat

William Pickle - Daily News columnist

George Scrubbs - Daily News photographer

Seth Surrey - Daily News editor

Pendleby - assistant to Winston Attle

Winston Attle - director Empire Survey Branch

General Goad - military administrator

The Rainbow Orchid: *the story so far...*

Lord Reginald Lawrence has entered into a wager with secretive businessman Urkaz Grope over who can do best in an annual orchid competition. At stake is the Trembling Sword of Tybalt Stone, and with it the Lawrence family's rights to the Stone estate, of which they have been guardians since the fifteenth century.

When *Daily News* reporter William Pickle reveals Grope has a secret weapon, the previously unknown black pearl orchid, Lawrence hires Julius Chancer, protégé of historical researcher Sir Alfred Catesby-Grey, to find a flower equally as fantastic – the legendary rainbow orchid. Uncertain if it exists or is just a myth, Julius, along with Lawrence's film-star daughter Lily and her agent Nathaniel Crumpole, fly to India to begin their search. They are hotly pursued by Grope's 'dark angel', Evelyn Crow, intent on preventing their success at any cost.

In India, Julius meets the impossibly old Father Pinkleton who claims they will find the rainbow orchid if they accompany his retainer, the mysterious Meru, back to his homeland somewhere in the uncharted reaches of the Hindu Kush mountains.

Back in England, William Pickle has been kidnapped by Urkaz Grope and his shadowy Order of the Black Lion. Meanwhile government agency the Empire Survey Branch attempt to persuade Sir Alfred Catesby-Grey to follow Julius and help find the rainbow orchid, though it appears they may have an ulterior motive . . .

Somewhere in the valleys of Chitral, Evelyn Crow and her henchmen catch up with Julius and friends, and in the ensuing fight Nathaniel Crumpole is lost over the edge of a precipitous cliff. Does this mean triumph for Urkaz Grope and the end of the quest for the rainbow orchid?

Ooh, my head...

Hm.

Abuij e Baba! Tay s'is' suais e?

I'm sorry, I don't...
Er, where am I?

Tay anora kay shiaw tik. Adhek hasi his e, baba?

Um...do you
speak English?

Ajo ticak takla
jhonel day! Pari
la, c'as'a zhe
ja' au oni!

Ug pi aas e?

Isa shilak hawa ajat hiu!

Oh! There's Julius!

1

Lily! You're up and about at last!

Where have you been? Where are we?

You had a fever, it's been over a week. Probably the shock... um, do you remember what happened? I mean, you know... Nathaniel?

Oh... yes. Yes, I do.

I thought it might have been a bad dream.

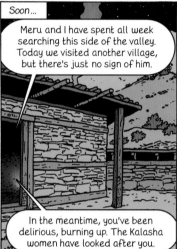

Soon...

Meru and I have spent all week searching this side of the valley. Today we visited another village, but there's just no sign of him.

In the meantime, you've been delirious, burning up. The Kalasha women have looked after you.

Julius, we've got to find Nat. We can't leave his... his body here... lost.

If we want to get down into the gully, where he fell, the only safe route is to cross the valley, but they say it's a week's journey.

There's no question. We have to.

What about the rainbow orchid? Will you continue?

I'm sorry, Meru. After what happened to Nat, I'm not sure I can. I just want to find him and take him home.

Next morning...

Will you be all right, Meru?

It is not an easy journey to make alone, but I do understand. I wish you good fortune to find Nathaniel.

Khamakha tay au zhuel'i hiw takla apaw des!

Koshan thi pari.

Khodayar baba.

Meru, how do I say thank you in Kalasha?

Hm. Mimi bo gudas aris will do.

Mimi bo gudas aris!

Warek deshaw moc in day!

Wareg asta angris ita aan!

Oh! It... it can't be!

Nat? I can't believe it!

Hey, kiddo!

How...? whu...you...you're alive!

Yup, I think so! Ha ha!

All right, Jules?

Well, yes!

I...I don't understand. Why are you here? And Nathaniel! How...?

It was a jam all right!

The Afridi and I took a tumble over the edge and I thought I was headed for the big one!

...Down we went, holding on to each other like the Dolly Sisters...

...Then there was a jolt and an almighty rip! My co-pilot's robe snagged a branch and that was him zotzed...

...Still, it put the brakes on for me and it wasn't far from there to splash down.

But I couldn't swim! The jolt had dislocated my arm, and as the water rushed me away, well, I guess I must have passed out...

...Next thing I know, I'm being hauled out by the mountain folk, put in a barn with the goats, fed, watered, and that's pretty much the crop until old Sir Alfred turned up. That was a spin!

We'd landed at Lahore and were making enquiries where to find you when we heard about a European discovered injured at the foot of the Lowari Pass.

The description made us think it was you, Julius.

So up we went and there was Nathaniel, looking somewhat the worse for wear. Mr Drubbin here put his Branch training to good use and reset the dislocated arm.

A very satisfying pop!

The Branch? You mean the Empire Survey Branch?

Yes indeed. Forgive me, this is Mr Drubbin. The money-men want the Branch closed down, but there's a chance to save it if we can impress them.

If, for instance, we can find the rainbow orchid.

Then our search for the orchid is back on!

WOOHOO! We're going to find the rainbow orchid!

It seems they intend to go on. Blast it.

That's it then. Still, what chance they'll actually find their stupid flower?

None. We're going to make certain of that.

Then we'll have to catch them on their way home. Right now we need to get you some proper treatment for that gunshot wound.

I'm fine. It's patched up, the bleeding's stopped, and anyway, out here's our best chance. We have to take it.

You can't be serious! You're not up to going any further, it'll kill you. We're going back.

We have our orders from Grope and we'll carry them out. At any cost!

You're deranged, Evelyn Crow. Stay here then. Die in the mountains. I'm going.

How dare you defy me! I'm in charge!

CHAK!

Hurgh!

THUD!

Foof!

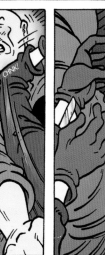

CHK!

THK!

Why did you make me do that? You shouldn't have made me do that!

Knife...Coward...can't face up to a fair fight...

Where's my hat?...I'm going...going home now...

Thunk!

Ah, drat! Wound's opened up again. Why did he make me do that! Idiot!

I've met you before, Meru, haven't I? You were Pinkleton's retainer, in Lahore, but you didn't speak any English then.

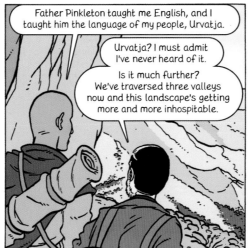

Father Pinkleton taught me English, and I taught him the language of my people, Urvatja.

Urvatja? I must admit I've never heard of it.

Is it much further? We've traversed three valleys now and this landscape's getting more and more inhospitable.

It has been many years since I walked this route, but there is...

look out!

TCHOM!

Kisssh!!!

That was close! What on earth caused that?

It was timed to perfection, right on top of us!

Rock falls happen all the time. We must be careful.

Thank you, Meru, you had your wits about you there.

Everything all right, Mr Drubbin?

Yes... certainly, Miss Lawrence. Just keeping an eye out.

You see that peak? *I-Palaka* - the guardian. Beyond that is a little-known trail that leads to *Uskandagadri*, the pass to my homeland.

6

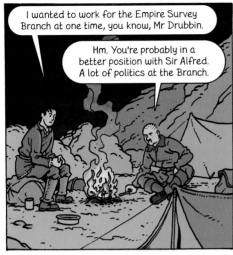

I wanted to work for the Empire Survey Branch at one time, you know, Mr Drubbin.

Hm. You're probably in a better position with Sir Alfred. A lot of politics at the Branch.

Will finding the rainbow orchid really prevent the War Office from shutting you down?

For a bit, maybe. Past glories – that's what they want. A little flare before they turn the lights out.

Why don't you turn in? I'll keep watch.

I'm sure you don't have to. I can't imagine there's anyone out here!

Just my nature, Mr Chancer. Good night.

And another day dawns...

Just a minute...

What's up, Sir Alfred?

Look!

Look up!

Is it a Buddha?

Look at those pictographs, just like at Mohenjo-daro!

Julius, Sir Alfred... I do believe we are being followed.

What? Are you sure?

If there's one person who's an expert in following people, it's Mr Drubbin.

And if there's anyone following us, it can only be one person – Evelyn Crow! Though I can hardly believe it.

Can I suggest that Mr Chancer and I slip behind some rocks to wait and see. The rest of you carry on. Keep the noise up.

It would be best to make sure. Be careful.

We'll catch you up.

Soon...

Won't even...sniff a buttercup, Mr...Grope...

Isn't this going a little too far? And where are your cronies?

Abandoned, eh? Turn back, Miss Crow. Go to your master and tell him you've failed.

Not return... or...any other flower...

She doesn't look too good, does she?

Woah there! She's wounded, it must be from Nathaniel's gunshot.

...a buttercup... Chancer...not even a buttercup...

Watch out!

Yargh!

Crafty girl, very crafty.

Nnf!

SMAK!

Hurgh!

She's not going to last long out here. I suggest we leave her to the elements and catch up with the others.

We can't leave her, Mr Drubbin! We'll have to bring her along.

This woman has done nothing but her best to kill you! She's the lowest of the low, not to be trusted!

And if we leave her to die, we are no better than she is!

We'll make a stretcher, we can pull it along. A bit of canvas from my tent... you cut some of those branches.

It's all very well having principles, Mr Chancer, but they'll let you down eventually. Ah well, if we must!

8

England...

Aaaa-CHOO!

Please try not to make any noise, Mr Scrubbs! We must attract as little attention as possible.

Right. Dressed up like a medieval Santa Claus! Anyway, it's your fault for making me meet you in the pouring rain the other day.

Newton, you still haven't explained where we're going, why we're dressed in this absurd get-up, or what our plan is to rescue William Pickle! I presume there is a plan?

Just trust me and do as I say. Put the mask on, we're here. Remember, don't attract attention.

What is this? The place is crawling with Santa Clauses!

There's normally only two guards here, escape would be impossible. Today's our day.

What is the password, please?

Leonore.

Thank you, brothers. You may enter.

What's everyone waiting for?

Stay close and don't talk to anyone. We have to wait for the right moment to get down into the cellar.

Good morning, brother! Are you on the council?

Er ... yes? Am I? I think so!

Me too! I'm in law enforcement. Put a villain away at least once a day, that's what I always say! Haw haw! What's your discipline, brother?

Well, er, brother...I'm in, um, news!

No, no, we're just lay members! Thank you, sorry to bother you!

Are you addressing me, brother?

No, no, brother! Don't mind us!

Wait a minute! He said he was on the Council! You can't impersonate a Council member!

What was that?

I wasn't talking to you!

Did you mean me? It's so hard to tell!

Here he is!

Urkaz Grope, the Grand Lion!

Grope?!

Shut up!

Greetings brothers! Greetings on this auspicious day, a new dawn, the inaugural meeting of the Eighth Council of the Order of the Black Lion, the first in over four hundred years!

BLACK LIONS!

RAAAARGH!

Brothers, in 1335 the First Council came together. For generations the Gropes stood proudly alongside the Grand Lion. We stayed loyal even during the Usurper's Council of 1377! And how were we rewarded? Why, a Lawrence was named Grand Lion and my ancestors were forgotten! Is that right?

BLACK LIONS!

RAAAARGH!

Raa!

When the Trembling Sword of Tybalt Stone fills this scabbard, and it will soon be mine, then I, Urkaz Grope, descendant of Sir Artus Grope, can legitimately claim the lands of Stone, and our Order will take its rightful place in its rightful home.

BLACK LIONS!

RAAAARGH!

Raaaargh!

And then comes our work. The gathering of wealth as we see fit, and a brotherhood united in infiltrating authority, until we, ourselves, become authority! You, my council, my brothers, my Black Lions...

RAAAARRGH!

Well, yes, that's the spirit. Now, let us celebrate. Let us plan. And practise the secret handshake. Remember, thumbs up!

Now's our chance. Come on, before someone wants to practise their handshake on you!

What on earth was all that? Who are those people?

Believe me, Mr Scrubbs, you'd rather not know. People of influence mixed with people from the gutter - a recipe for disaster if you ask me.

Pickle should be in here...

Hee hee! He's in for a big surprise!

Ding!

Awrgh!

10

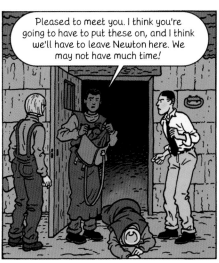

11

Is this the best way?

I don't know! Keep going!

What about George? We can't just leave him!

You suggest we go back and get him? I'll see you later then.

There they are!

Agh!

Oww! My ankle!

Go on!

Steps up to the road! I'm going to make it!

PICKLE!

On the count of three I'll give the order to snap her neck. Give yourself up and she gets to remain upright!

One...two...

SLAM!

I don't know how you found us, Mr Scrubbs, but I have my suspicions. In the meantime, I'll have to decide whether holding you is any longer of use to me. I rather think not. Goodbye.

Newton must have woken up and slipped away. But he'll try again, won't he?

Not after that disaster. No, I'm afraid I think our fate rests entirely on the whim of that megalomaniac madman, Urkaz Grope!

The seventh day in the mountains...

Are you all right, Lily?

I can't feel my feet. They're almost numb from the cold!

Meru! Where are we?

We are close. This is *Uskandagadri!* Once through the pass we will be out of the snow.

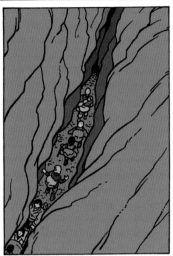

This isn't going to work, we'll have to take her off the stretcher.

Um...I think I'm stuck.

Wow, look at that!

The temperature through here is much higher, can you feel it?

We seem to have entered some kind of temperate pocket. Look at the mist coming off the water...it's warm!

Still alive, is she?

There's a pulse. Just about, anyway.

Some of these surface rocks are vesicular. Incredible! I wouldn't expect to find such blatant remnants of volcanic activity up here. What an oddity!

Well! And here's another surprise! Julius...what do you make of this?

15

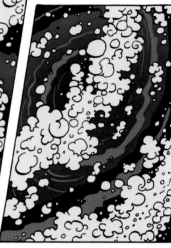

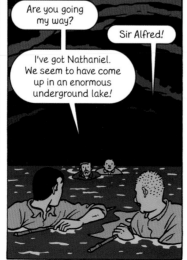

Some time later...

Hey, the water's getting cooler, don't you think?

And isn't the current speeding up a bit?

How much further, Meru? I'm exhausted!

I don't know, these tunnels are unknown to me but... ah, I see light up ahead!

Yes, I see it!

No whirlpools this time I hope!

No, it should... oh, no... I've just realised...

Ho-jee!

What can we do?

Swim to the side!

We're going too fast!

Hold on!

AAAAGGGHHHH

Yah! No more water! No more aeroplanes! Just dry, solid land from now on!

Avrisana! Okthari avrilak yovantu syan!

17

Wait ... jarma! Zakaam tu aham mabhava te zorata! Jarma!

So this is your homeland, Meru?

This is Urvatja. Come, I will show you.

Soon ...

This heat is something! My clothes are practically dry already!

It's strange... some kind of geothermal effect.

Look at that!

Remember the seals at Mohenjo-daro? Mr Banerji's unicorns!

Incredible. A completely unknown species!

What crops are growing over there?

It is *tilu*, a kind of sesame.

We seem to have come to a dead end ...

No, there's a track leading down. Does that go to your village, Meru?

My village? Well ...

...not my village exactly.

Oh!

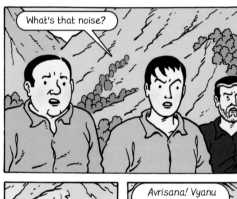

What's that noise?

Avrisana! Vyanu mitaa zirvana!

Fl... flying... it's flying!

Tu syan chaldhi te yovo, Meru. Eska si otu domasti na patha.

Upjanu, aham isti avgatu te sasti mi alaph. Bahu prabesh isti kranta.

I'm not feeling particularly welcome, Meru...

They are wary of strangers. I just need to explain...

Stay away from me, you rampallion!

Mr Drubbin! Please...

VASTAVAA!

Don't...   uh!

Fsss!

Fsss!

Fsss!

No!

Fsss!   Fsss!

Stop! Mr Drubbin! We need to...

KRAK!

Ah!

Fsss!

Shtop... op...

Fsss!

Julius? Julius? Can you hear me?

Sir Alfred? Has... has Charlotte made breakfast?

I think your brain needs to catch up. Have a look.

Kuthi si Meru, te tasaya sinti ki doozeka, yovo-a te abhigar kristaa!

Ah... ah, yes.

Did I see... that thing, was it flying?

Yes, you saw it. I think we may have witnessed something like a vimana, one of the mythical aerial chariots mentioned in the Mahabharata.

And the connection with Mohenjo-daro...

Parus! Na zorata!

Ki moodaka si kuthi. Mahiku, navu satja-i mahaa tharanii Madsha si migata vasatja eska naru!

Zirvana, Upjanu. I-Dokrista ka niztu, mitaa tharanii ka kristuu.

What do you think's happening?

I have no idea, but it doesn't appear to be going well for Meru. And therefore maybe us too.

Do you think Meru didn't tell us quite everything?

BWOOOOOOOOORRR!

Saydima Makshjia!

BWOOOOOOOOOORRR!

20

Makshjia ...

Parus, moodaka!

Mahaa tharanii, yovo-a si ki doozeka te Urvatja. Migatu he kristaa aham upagodi.

Mahaa tharanii, I dokrista trebizam niztu aham upagodi. Zekomi ov mananu.

Dokrista.

Not long after ...

Phirati dah!

Well, it's not the worst prison in the world.

There's a window at least.

He sakana atithi satja Makshjia tu syan. Iikzana anu tu kav.

Same to you! No idea what you're saying, Mack.

High Strategos Upjanu says you are guests of Great Makshjia, our queen. You will be well treated.

Did he mention anything about dinner?

21

I am Majaa. You are welcome to Urvatja.

What about our friend, Meru? What's happened to him?

He will see his fate in the court. I am sorry he is your friend for he will most possibly bear death for his crimes.

His crimes?

Then it is unknown to you that Meru is responsible for the death of the son of Great Nahatha, our queen before Great Makshjia, as well as other traitorous events upon his people.

Where did you learn our language, Majaa?

My father... ah, here he arrives!

Forgive my delay, honoured guests! I trust my daughter has looked well after you. I am Gozavu, the Keeper.

Kipper?

Keeper — of the affairs of Urvatja, past and to come.

Oh. Well now I'm thinking of kippers. That's my tummy gurgling!

But... what is Urvatja? Who are you?

I would show you the laastra, stone tablets that speak our history, but I am sorry you cannot leave this chamber, for now, at least.

Stone tablets? Carved with images, about this big?

Nay, the laastra are as tall as bakku, our story was written for the gods! It may be that smaller copies were made, our history told by those who stayed...

Uha, I shall tell...

The laastra does speak of the three lands ruled by the goddess, whose name is now lost.

We left our homelands to share our great knowledge in the world. The Agva and Ukkha went westward, and we, the Urvah, came to the valley you now call Indoos.

Mohenjo-daro!

Uha, Mohenjo was built upon the ruins of Dagalha, a great city, by descendants who had forgotten our ways after Mahaa Migaka, the Great Doom.

Great Doom? What happened?

Resapho
minava.

Na daha, gurasanti. Yovo!

Yuh!

Makshjia!

Tu trebizam achda, Meru. Upjanu ka tasati sthita satja otu migatu.

Sayu hoha mi oochaya, Makshjia. Ki daivaa so-i atva satja esku. Aham kahav tu nimaa.

Karima zoratay eska. Tu trebizam iistra eska bhava.

Tu trebizam iistra otu domasti uta arakav ki nivo taan.

Djaph sakana, Meru. He ahama, muktva otu bhava uta achda.

24

I don't know what this is, but it's delicious! I wonder if we could take some back with us?

You think they'll let us leave? I somehow doubt that.

Sure they will! That Mr Gozavu is a genuine bean. Honoured guests he called us!

Yes, honoured by two armed guards right outside this room. We need a plan, starting with getting rid of those guards...

...Unless you think they're just going to suddenly fly away and let us...

KA-THUMP!

CRASH!

Meru...?

Kari ma...

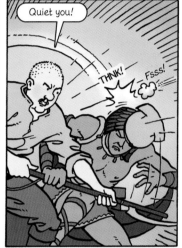

Quiet you!

THNK!

Fsss!

Yaa!

CHK!

Fsss!

Uh!

Thank you, Mr Drubbin.

We must go. Staying here will be dangerous.

Well, now it will! We were being looked after quite nicely, thank you!

I'm certain you were. But Upjanu will not tolerate your presence for long, and he will not allow you to leave either, trust me.

I'd like to trust you, Meru, but we've been told you're a traitor and a murderer. Look at the situation you've led us into! You owe us an explanation.

I do, but not now. We must...

Meru!

Meru escaped! PALAKU! UHKTA SI MERU!

Zirvana, Gozavu! Please...

All right! All right... I will explain. Please, Gozavu, zek ahama zoratu.

Zora anam!

25

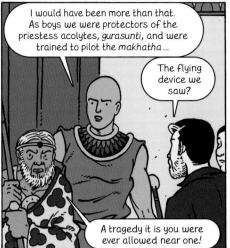
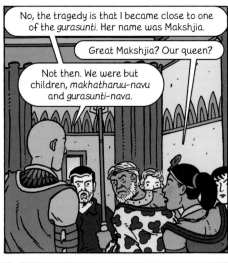
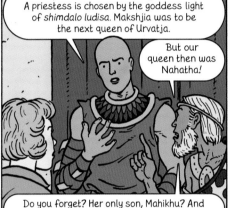

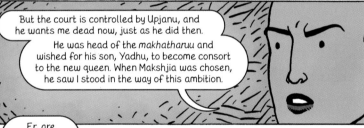

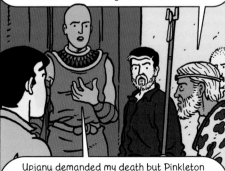

Yet you have returned.

It was Pinkleton's dying wish. He persuaded me things would have changed...but they have not.

Upjanu now heads the council and he will have me dead before any trial takes place.

It does not seem possible. Makshjia is a good queen.

I believe Meru, father. Why has not a new queen been chosen from the *gurasunti-nava*? The council delay it. It keeps Yadhu as consort and Upjanu in dominance.

Makshjia, Great Makshjia, has no real power, and you hold no influence with her, Gozavu. Long ago the goddess left our lands. And now I leave too - forever.

And exactly how do you plan to get us all out of here?

This key is our way out of Urvatja. You seem comfortable with the dart spear, Mr Drubbin, how does the rest of a guard's attire suit you?

Now this sounds more like the kind of plan I was thinking of!

Meru, this *shimdalo ludisa*... the rainbow orchid - is there any way we can get to it? We're so close!

There is not enough time. You would need to go...Hm, I wonder... But there may be a way...

Gozavu Arasaptalik, you could be of help to me.

Then if I can, *Meru Makhatharuu*, I will.

You know of *Urvaa-dar*?

The abandoned hill temple?

It is where Makshjia and I would long ago secretly meet, and it is where we must go to now.

I will go on ahead, but there is one thing I would ask of my homeland – *paani devatu*, water of the goddess. Go to the cavern, and fetch some. Take everyone with you, then come by way of the chamber tunnels.

Julius, you must take what you need there.

Er, what about Crow? She can't be carried through this place in a big crowd. How about Majaa and I take her separately. Gives us a better chance.

I don't know if that's a good idea...

Uha. While you collect the water for Meru, we can go through the lower corridors. It is a shorter way to carry her.

That's settled then!

Very well. You must all be at *Urvaa-dar* before the sun sets upon the crown of *Iisha*.

Now, take care and let us go!

Good luck!

Gone. Good.

The only danger will be when we are outside. To reach the foot of the hills there may be one or two of the guard by that path.

Well, you can leave her, she can stay and rot. I've got a different path in mind now.

What is this?

The Great Library, the records. You're taking me there instead.

I do not understand...

You don't have to, just do it or you're going to come to serious harm. Now move!

27

Soon ...

Majaa, resaphao satja-i zivasa.

Tetu mi resapho.

Don't try anything, Majaa. I mean it.

clik!

These are the laastra satja-i Mahaa Migaka. They depict the destruction that caused the mother river to dry, and farms to become barren desert. The Great Doom.

Ha! To think the best I thought I'd see was some faded relief on a crumbling old ruin! Attle will be delighted.

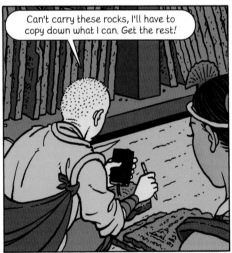

Can't carry these rocks, I'll have to copy down what I can. Get the rest!

The others do not know of this, is that so?

And they won't find out, especially from you. Now pile them up! Anything showing weapons, fighting, death ... that kind of thing ...

These are useless to you. Such machines cannot now be made.

Oh, I'm sure we'll get something out of them. You'd be surprised what we're capable of at the Branch ...

No one understands them. Perhaps, even, they are but a myth.

You think I want to make war? I want to prevent war! I fought at the Somme and saw all my mates dead in a day - my own Great Doom! With the ultimate weapon in the hands of the British Empire, there will be no more war, no more Sommes!

You might believe that, but what of those that come after? They will not know your Somme. If such a weapon exists, it will one day be used. It will destroy not just your warriors, it will destroy your world.

Yagh! Enough waffle! I need to get these down ...

It's getting hotter the further we descend!

We will soon be within *Ilukajanu*, the chamber discovered by our ancestors when they first came to this place.

Flowing lava! I suspected there was something volcanic within the valley, but an actual live volcano?

Yet one we have tamed. The first settlers did make these channels. The power beneath the mountain gives Urvatja its life!

These are the priest kings of old, from before the Great Doom. Araxathamu was the last, who did lead our people here.

And here is the spring of the goddess. Her name may now be forgotten, but she has not abandoned her children. *Mi devatu aham tu kahav.*

Fill this *ankhu* skin, it will last Meru a good while.

Ju...Julius...Am I looking at what I think I'm looking at?

Oh...my... goodness...

It's the orchid! The rainbow orchid!

It's like glass... transparent yet soft, organic!

Is this the one Pinkleton found?

Uha, on the slopes of *Iisha-ziknu.*

Some say Araxathamu discovered *shimdalo ludisa* in the valley, a sign from the goddess of our new home. Others believe our ancestors brought it with them, a flower transmuted by the weapons of the Great Doom.

That fits the narrative on the stone tablets!

Well never mind all that! How do we move this thing? Anyone got a flower pot?

You... you intend to take it?!

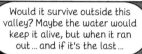
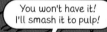

Argh! All right! I've had enough.

What have you done to Mr Drubbin? Where is he?

Ha!

Fwip!

Nnnnk!

You must be the most naïve fool I've ever met!

As for Drubbin, he had his own plans. Sounded pretty interesting too!

Thonk!

Woah!

KTHUMP!

Aaaggh! Help! Help! The lava! I'm slipping!

Are you sure you need help? I don't want you to think I'm being naïve.

I can't hold on, Chancer! Please! PLEASE!

Hm! It does look quite hot down there.

Save me! I'll tell you...I'll tell you about Grope! His orchid! I can't hold on!

His orchid? Go on then.

The black orchid's a fake! Newton...he...he's a flower colourist!

He's got a contraption that sits under the roots feeding it some kind of special ink he invented...AGH! I'm going...grab me...

GRAB ME!

skriiit!

Failure! I've failed! I always thought I'd choose death first... I'm a coward!

Oh, don't be so hard on yourself. Come on, let's get down...

I don't deserve to live!

Evelyn, no!

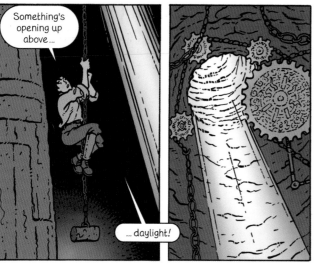

See! There is *Urvaa-dar!* It is not far now.

What is that place? Will it lead us out of here?

It is an old mountain shrine, abandoned long before my time. It may be that Meru knows of a passage within that leads to the mountains outside.

I don't see Meru anywhere...

What's happening?

Earthquake! The volcano! It's going to blow!

Look at the shrine!

It's ... it's rising!

FWUMF!

Makhatha! It is *makhatha!*

Yes Gozavu! Long abandoned *makhatha* of the disbanded Priest Guard, then a forgotten mountain shrine for *Gak* herders. Now come! We must be away!

Where's Drubbin got to?

Here he comes! Look!

They're coming! Behind us!

Oh crikey! We'd better move it!

Get in that thing!

I've got a strong feeling of deja-vu!

Is this thing safe?

What happened? Evelyn found us, she said ...

They saw us leaving the palace! Majaa overheard the guards ... that Upjanu bloke told everyone Meru escaped to murder the queen. We're to be killed on sight! Hurry!

33

Do not let him take his book!

Majaa?

Babata, sayu ista ki hoshja tasatu satja laastra satja-i Mahaa Migaka!

Don't listen to her! Quick! Help me up! They're here!

Drutachda yovantu syan!

Majaa! Let go!

Yava esku tu trebizam ma!

Majaa!

Chaliba saya!

Fsss! Fsss! Fsss! Fsss!

Agh! Take... take to Attle...

Drubbin!

Makhatha jarmaha i ugadri esku!

Eeeah!

Mi khahav vilasa, Meru.

England, Pitscally House...

I suppose we can't put it off any longer. There's been no word since the telegram at Karachi.

I'm sure Miss Lily is perfectly fine, sir.

I do hope you're right, Perkins, though with no sign of this mythical rainbow orchid I fear we have nothing good enough to prevent Grope from winning the competition, the sword, the estate...

Oh, really, what's the point?

We have our dignity, sir! Now look, *Miltonia spectabilis* is looking particularly fine at the moment.

Yes, I suppose so. What about *Catasetum macrocarpum*? A very perky leaf.

Though *Huntleya wallisii* has a good colour on it. I can't decide.

Sir, if I may, I'm rather fond of the *Paphiopedilum*. It's responded quite exceptionally this year.

What a decision.

Nellie, what do you say? Which one do you like?

Ooh no, sir! I don't know any of the fancy names!

But which one do you like the look of? The casting vote is yours!

Well... erm, they're all so lovely, but I think... I think that one. It's sort of simple but beautiful, if you know what I mean.

Ah, what an eye you have, Nellie! Could there be anything better to stand against Grope's black orchid than a white orchid?

Perkins, prepare *Phalaenopsis aphrodite* for the Wembley Exhibition.

While a few miles away...

Careful! Keep it level... please!

Do stop fussing, Newton. I've planned everything to the last detail, it's perfectly safe.

You know they display the winner for a week afterwards, Mr Grope. The black orchid won't last a day without my constant attention!

I won't allow it to be displayed. As soon as I've won, it'll be destroyed. I don't like evidence hanging around.

But... but that orchid is my greatest work! You can't destroy it! The hours I've spent...

The money *I've* spent! It's mine, Newton. You're mine! Everything's mine!

Ha ha. Think of the prize money, my friend. That'll be yours, all of it! You'll be able to afford that trip to the Amazon you talked about. Once you've paid all your debts, of course.

Now, go and make sure that crate's secure. Good man!

I can't wait to be rid of that insufferable gudgeon. Still, he'll be joining his precious orchid in a couple of days. Is everything in place, Scobie, just in case his disappearance is noticed?

It is, Mr Grope. A few documents, a couple of witnesses if we need them. The usual.

Good, good. Now, let's go and win this silly competition so I can start calling myself the Earl of Baggall as soon as possible! Then the serious work can begin!

Wembley...

Ladies and gentleman, welcome to the Fifth British Empire Exhibition!

Within a matter of hours you can travel the length and breadth of our wonderful Empire, from Canada to Australia, Hong Kong to Africa, and meet kinsmen from all our great dominions!

At two o'clock, in the stadium, witness the Ninth Lancers re-enact the Battle of Arghandi, and marvel as the Reverend Adams saves five cavalrymen to win the Victoria Cross!

Ooh, is that extra?

A mere thruppence, madam.

Over there, the Palaces of Arts and Industry, down there, the Amusement Park, and on this side, Treasure Island and the Gold Coast Railway! But let us begin our tour with a trip to India!

The India Pavilion, with its slender towers and graceful minarets, bears witness to the genius of Mughal architecture!

I say! That's dashed interesting. Look up there!

A treasure house of mysticism decorated with splashing fountains and filled with rare perfumes. Dine in style in the Maharaja Restaurant...

What is that thing?

Ooh! It's marvellous!

My... my goodness me!

Amazing what British engineering can do these days. Very clever!

Why don't they tell me when they add new attractions!

Must be a hydrogen balloon, it's not that amazing.

Is it a ride?

Um... well... that depicted, er, the myth of the gods of India, in their, um... sky chariots...

Excuse me, which way to the Botanical Exhibition?

Oh, er, you want the Horticulture Garden, that way, past the orchestra stand and turn right at the ostrich paddock.

Thanks!

My legs are feeling rather wobbly!

It is today, isn't it?

Yes! Definitely today! I think.

Hello, Mr Palfrey! Sounding magnificent!

Sir Alfred!

Down here! There's the Horticulture Garden!

Oh! Lily Lawrence! I... I'm afraid they started without you ...

Go and fetch a policeman. Right now, it's an emergency!

TODA
ORCHI
COMPETITI

Stop! That orchid is a fake!

What is this? Who are you?

Lily?

Urkaz Grope's black orchid is artificially coloured. That man, Newton, is an expert flower dyer!

Wh... wh... This is preposterous!

Don't you dare lay a finger on that! It's extremely delicate!

I hope you didn't lie to me, Evelyn Crow ...

That doesn't look regulation!

Did someone here ask for the police?

I'll deal with this, officers! I'm Detective Inspector Starling. Now, what's going on here?

I've been had, Inspector! This man sold me the black orchid as a genuine spectacle, now it turns out it's a sham! Arrest him this instant!

What? No!

37

Nice try, *Grope*, but how are you going to explain the disappearance of William Pickle, the *Daily News* reporter?

And Eloise Tayaut!

Yes! And I can tell you where they're being kept! The sea-front cottage down at Little Trilling! I'll tell you everything!

What?! Kidnapping too? You asked to borrow my holiday cottage so your ailing mother could get some sea air, but instead you use it for yet more criminal activity! I'll bet you don't even have an ailing mother!

Holiday cottage? Mother?! No, no... I don't! I mean...

I knew it!

This will never stand! I've got nothing to do with kidnapping, or that cottage!

Scobie? Have you anything to add? Eh?

Eh?!

Uh? Oh, yes, sir. Both the postman and the, um, dairy maid in Little Trilling informed me they saw Newton and, er, strange goings-on at the cottage. They'll provide statements, I have no doubt.

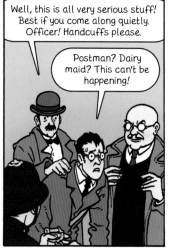

Well, this is all very serious stuff! Best if you come along quietly. Officer! Handcuffs please.

Postman? Dairy maid? This can't be happening!

I'm very disappointed in you, Newton.

Inspector, I hope he'll get a fair trial.

Of course, sir. I expect Judge Findlay would sit for such a case.

Perfect! Well, you've solved the case, Inspector. Good work!

Thank you, sir. Put a villain away at least once a day, that's what I always say! *Haw haw!*

I don't believe this!

Constable! That flower is evidence, bring it along!

Right you are, sir.

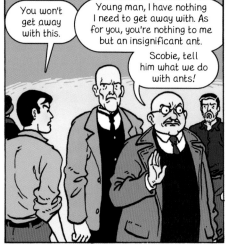

You won't get away with this.

Young man, I have nothing I need to get away with. As for you, you're nothing to me but an insignificant ant. Scobie, tell him what we do with ants!

Well... the best method I've found is a heap of baking soda mixed in with pinches of mint and lavender, plus some cinnamon if I can get it...

No! No! *Idiot!* We crush ants! Crush without mercy! *Tch!* Come on!

Sir Alfred, what about Eloise? If Grope gets down to that cottage first...

Hmm. He seems to have framed Newton quite nicely for all that, but just in case...

Officer, I need you to put a telephone call through to the police sergeant down at Little Trilling. Tell him to get over to the cottage on the sea front right away.

Uh, I think I'd better ask Inspector Starling first, sir...

You'll do no such thing. Now, I happen to be on very good terms with Chief Inspector Watling at the Yard. Do as I say, then come and find us at the main entrance.

We'll get down to Trilling and it'll be your name on the report for freeing the captives.

Right! I'll get to it, sir!

Ahem! This is a most unusual situation, ladies and gentlemen, but I have consulted with my colleagues, Mr Farfathom of the Royal Horticultural Society, and Lady Drimpley-Gore of the Amateur Orchid Growers' Council of Great Britain, and we have agreed to invoke rule 53, sub-clause 2.

Therefore, the black pearl orchid is disqualified on grounds of forgery, and all remaining entrants move up one place.

Miss Daphne Sprigg now takes the Certificate of Merit for *Miltonia flava*. Mr A. Harris is awarded the bronze medal for *Gongora maculata*. The silver medal goes to the Reverend Checkington for a fine *Serapias occultata*...

...And first prize, the Wembley Botanical Trophy, is awarded to Lord Reginald Lawrence for his *Phalaenopsis aphrodite*, a reminder that simple beauty can often be just as stunning as the most ornate and colourful *Orchidaceae*.

Miss Lawrence, as our special guest, would you be so kind as to do the honours?

Oh, yes... certainly!

I'm delighted to present first prize in the orchid competition of the fifth Wembley Botanical Exhibition to Lord Lawrence for his beautiful *Phal...* um, *phlalanops...* er, white orchid!

Well done, father.

The Stone estate is saved! Thank you, thank you!

And so...

The main entrance is back the way we came, by the India Pavilion.

I'm looking forward to seeing Mr Pickle again. I've one or two things to say to him about stirring up this whole affair!

Come to think of it, I need to give Winston Attle a piece of my mind too, but he'll have to wait.

Julius, Sir Alfred, thank you. You may not have come back with the rainbow orchid, but it's thanks to you, and my Lily, that the Stone Estate remains with the Lawrence family where it rightfully belongs.

Just promise me, Lord Lawrence, no more card games with rich, scheming businessmen!

Oh! *Ha ha!* Yes, indeed. There's a lesson, eh?

Thank you for everything, Jules.

Oh!

Couldn't have done it without you, Lily.

Um, I hope we can meet up again...

Definitely!

Maybe I'll see you when you collect your car, though Nat wants to rush back to Hollywood with his new film idea, and I've got *Melody of Life* to shoot. You should come out there, I can show you behind the scenes!

Oh... yeah, that would be great.

I know it was dangerous, but it was an amazing experience! It's inspired Nat's film idea. You'll be in it, played by Buddy Rogers or someone! *Ha ha!* I'll play me, of course. I think United Players might give Nat a chance this time!

Nathaniel! Come and tell Julius...

Nat! What are you doing?!

40

The Empire Survey Branch, Milton Square...

Anything with 'unknown origin' on the tag, pack it up for Section-D.

Section-D? Is that storage?

No, Attle, that's auction. We have to try and claw back some of the money we poured into this withered old museum of yours.

You're selling everything! Desecrating two hundred years of work! Sir Alfred was right about you lot. There's more value to what we do than mere profit, General Goad.

What you *did*, Attle. As of today, the Empire Survey Branch is defunct. Anyway, it's not everything... the Ashmolean has agreed to take the nice Egyptian stuff.

What about the military projects you diverted us on to when you took over? We were making real progress on research into the possibility of ancient superweapons.

Yes, biggest waste of the lot. We're keeping a couple of interesting bits and bobs, but there's already a buyer for most of it. Let's see... some physics instructor at the University of Berlin... Szilárd.

The Germans? You're selling our superweapon research to the Germans?!

It's twaddle. If they want to chase myths they can, and anything that sets Germany in the wrong direction gets a commendation in my book!

To think you wasted your final resources on such nonsense!

If you mean Mr Drubbin, he was not a resource. He was one of our finest agents... a good man.

What about Sir Alfred's report? What he discovered out there?

That man has his own agenda, always has. He could certainly give Rider Haggard a run for his money with such children's stories.

Ha ha! That's a good one, eh? Rider Haggard! Well, on with the show!

The offices of The Daily News...

A LEMONADE FACTORY?!

You're taking my story off the front page and replacing it with the opening of a lemonade factory?!

Not just the front page, Pickle, your piece won't appear at all. That Newton chap was convicted, it's old news. Now, I've got a nice little story for you, a stage magician...

It wasn't Newton! It was Grope! He put me in a cell with that French girl! George too! They wore masks like some kind of cult! I'm giving *The Daily News* a massive scoop!

Pickle, I'm glad you're safe and back with us, but I'm sorry, there's nothing I can do! The order comes from up on high. Your story's a dead duck.

Right! I QUIT!

I'm taking this to the *National News!* And they'll pay me more than I've ever got at this miserable rag!

The *National* won't take it! Your story's untouchable, Pickle!

Do you think Grope is behind this? How can he get to the papers?

Somehow he has. I might have to wait for the right moment, but Urkaz Grope won't get the better of William Pickle, no way!

Come on, George. There's plenty of other big stories out there for us to put our names on in the meantime. Let's go and find one!

The end.

Other Items

SENTENCE IN KIDNAPPING CASE

A sentence of two years' impris... was imposed by Mr. Justice Findlay... Old Bailey yesterday on Mr. W. New... botanist specialising in the dyeing... flowers, who had been found guilty a... trial extending over two days. He... charged with the kidnapping of Mr. Pickle of The Daily News, Mr.... Scrubbs, also of The Daily News, and... French airplane mechanic, Mlle. Taya... and keeping them locked at a remo... location in the village of Little Trilling o... the coast. Furthermore, he was charge... with defrauding and tainting the... reputation of upstanding businessman and... philanthropist, Mr. U. Grope, who brought... the charges in conjunction with the... Metropolitan Police.

Mr. Newton has a history of debt and... mixing with the less salubrious types of... society, a point that was noted by Mr.... Justice Findlay who also stated that Mr.... Newton was "guilty all over" and that... very little evidence was necessary to see... was guilty of the kidnapping of three... persons and the besmirching of the fine... Mr. Grope." The Judge directed the jury to... return a guilty verdict, and this was indeed... presented after just ten minutes... deliberation.

Blackwood's Edinburgh Magazine

1872.]

...but it can certainly be said of Richard... Grope that he was a man of rare... ability and loyalty, serving on the Grand... council under three of the Grand... Lions, namely John Tybalt Stone, the... doomed Henry Tybalt Stone, and... John Stone.

Artus Grope, Richard's son, took... his place at the table of the Fourth... Council in 1387 upon the death of his... father and appears to be the last of... the Gropes to have an association... with the Order.

By the time of the inauguration of... the Fifth Council, the Grope name... has disappeared from the ledgers,... and the Lawrence name has come to... prominence. When Hugo Stone died... without issue in 1445, it was... Carminus Lawrence who became the... Grand Lion of the Sixth Council and... inherited the Tybalt sword and the... Stone estate, which remains in the...

Lawrence family to... four-hundred years...

Carminus was... Henry Lawrence... Thomas, from who... in 1426 at the age o... years old. Five yea... Elizabeth, the dau... De Horsbroc, and... Humphrey Law... Humphrey would... Lion for the... seventh, in 1470...

There can be little doubt the... Lawrence family earned their status... on the Council thanks to the loyalty... shown by Henry in the affair of the... usurper, Geoffrey De Haven, in... 1377. The only known illustration of... the Order most likely dates from this... time and depicts John Stone, Richard... Grope – probably the figure standing... – and Henry Lawrence. The sword of...

concilium

BOBBY "THE BOX" BOSWELL

CLASSIC BRITISH PU...
THE ROMANY CHA...

Please Post in...

A plant and its own...
if :—

1. the plant has previ...
kind or from any Brit...

2. the plant is found to...
artificially enhanced o...
attributed...

3. the plant has not be...
the subscribed entrant...

UNKNOWN

slate 4

TAYAUT
AEROBATIC CIRCUS

TAYAUT

The NEW Fantastic
FLYING FURNACE
ONE WEEK ONLY

Hosted by Lord Reginald Lawrence at
The Stone Estate, Sussex

SPECTACULAR!

NATHANIEL
B. CRUMPOLE
PRESENTS

"FORGOTTEN
VALLEY
of the
ORCHID"

Starring
BUDDY ROGERS
LILY LAWRENCE
OLIVE BORDEN
JAMES PIERCE

*The biggest
adventure the
silver screen
has ever seen!*

UNITED
PLAYERS
PRODUCTION

United Players

FILMS OF THE WEEK

"FORGOTTEN VALLEY
OF THE ORCHID."

This American film is the first to come from the pen and mega-phone of director, Nathaniel B. Crumpole, previously known as the United Players publicity agent for British screen actress Miss Lily Lawrence. It will be no surprise, then, to find the film stars Miss Lawrence and that it has rolled right off the United Players lot. It is a barely-believable adventure yarn with a lot of silliness, but good fun all the same. Despite much life and movement throughout, the action is spread sparsely among the reels, though it is exciting enough when it comes. Olive Borden (much admired in "Sinners in Love") plays the evil queen of a forgotten Himalayan valley while Buddy Rogers ("Wings") is an unconvincing hero who spends most of the film saving various animals from absurd dangers (a tiger cub eventually joins them on their quest and goes on to save Lily from an impressively filmed lava flow). If pulp adventure is the new direction for Miss Lawrence, then we would advise against it – she is far more effective in the social dramas we know and love her for ("Melody of Life", "Little May") and "Forgotten Valley", despite entertaining as a matinée treat, would be a step down for one of her acting stature. Playing this week at the Paramount and Capitol theatres. —J. Bruton.